Gretchen OVER the BEACH

R. W. Alley

CLARION BOOKS
Houghton Mifflin Harcourt
Boston ◆ New York

Clarion Books
215 Park Avenue South
New York, New York 10003

Clarion Books is an imprint of Houghton Mifflin Harcourt Publishing Company.

www.hmhco.com

The illustrations in this book were done in ink, pencils, watercolors,
gouaches, and acrylics on Bristol board paper.
The text was set in Julius Primary.

Library of Congress Cataloging-in-Publication Data is available.
ISBN 978-0-547-90708-6

Manufactured in Malaysia
TWP 10 9 8 7 6 5 4 3 2 1
4500562718

With love to Z & C & M for
making my world so colorful

ONE breezy beach day, Gretchen's brothers and sister rushed down to the water. Gretchen called, "Wait up!"

But no one listened.

Not Annabelle.

Not Clark.

Not Mitchell.

When everyone else splashed into the waves,
Gretchen called, "Take me and the roly-polys with you!"
But no one listened.

Then Gretchen's sporty new hat
with the fancy ribbon
flew away with the breeze.

"Come back here!" she called.
But the hat didn't listen either.

Gretchen grabbed the ribbon.
The roly-polys grabbed Gretchen.

Gretchen caught the hat and scrambled on.

"Take us to the high clouds!" she said.
Now the hat listened.
Up and up they went.

When they reached the wispy wave-clouds, Gretchen dove in.

She was flying!

A little island cloud blew in on the breeze.
"Let's rest here," said Gretchen.
But oh, no! Where were the roly-polys?

Gretchen called to a passing gull,
"Have you seen my roly-polys?"
The gull had not.

So Gretchen told the gull
all about the roly-polys
and their amazing adventures.
The gull was all ears.

Suddenly . . .
a thundercloud
swallowed up the little island cloud.

Gretchen and the gull got away.
But what about the roly-polys?
Had they gotten away too?

Then, high, high, high
above the clouds,
Gretchen spotted the roly-polys!

"Hooray!" the roly-polys cheered.
"We knew you'd find us!"

But then the hat tipped.
Out tumbled the roly-polys!

"Gotcha!"

With her hat as a parachute,
Gretchen and the roly-polys drifted
down, down, down to the beach.

When the others returned
to shore, Annabelle said, "How
did you get so wet?"

Mitchell said, "You weren't
even in the big waves."

"Look," said Clark, "you've lost
the fancy ribbon from your new hat."

"Big clouds are better than big waves,"
said Gretchen.
And she wasn't a bit worried about her ribbon.